Shared Reading

Page to read **together** to introduce the story.

The animals on the farm were hungry.

The children liked to help Dad feed the animals.

Bella was hungry too.

BRAMBLE
BELLA

Milly liked to feed the cow.

"Moo, moo," said the cow.

cow liked to

WILLOW
BELLA

Ben liked to feed the pig.

“Oink, oink,” said the pig.

the pig liked

DAISY
B
BELLA

Kal liked to feed the sheep.

"Baa, baa," said the sheep.

sheep to the

PiPPA
BELLA

Don liked to feed the donkey.

“Hee haw,” said the donkey.

liked donkey the

BELLA

Milly liked to feed the calf.

"Moo, moo," said the calf.

Bella was hungry too.

hungry said was

BELLA

Milly fed Bella.

“Purr, purr,” said Bella.

Bella	said	Milly

POP it on!

cow

HELPING DAD

sheep

HELPING DAD

pig

HELPING DAD

donkey

HELPING DAD

said

HELPING DAD

the

HELPING DAD

was

HELPING DAD

to

HELPING DAD

Developing Language Skills

Use the following techniques to help develop your child's language.

Encouraging Naming within a Category

Encourage your child to give examples within a category already present, e.g. farm animals.

When you have finished reading the book with your child, encourage him to remember the animals in the story and to expand on the theme, e.g. naming other animals you might find on a farm (horse, chicken, dog, duck etc.).

Animal Sounds: after reading the book read it again with your child and encourage him to tell you the sound each animal makes. Help him to expand on this by introducing other possibilities, e.g. sounds made by horses, ducks etc.

Encouraging Word Associations

Extend your child's vocabulary by helping him to develop word associations with a word in the story, e.g. farm.

Encourage your child to talk about taking care of animals on a farm. Talk to him about what food each animal eats, where the animal might live (sty, pen, stable etc.). Also talk about what each animal gives us: milk from cows, wool from sheep, etc.

Talk to your child about what else farms produce, e.g. vegetables like potatoes and carrots, and cereals for our bread and breakfast. Talk about what he might find interesting on a farm, e.g. tractors, combine harvesters etc.

The POPS reading programme delivers a core vocabulary on everyday topics your child will need at home and at school. The topic(s) covered by this book are:

Animals

For further help, please download our free manual for Teachers and Parents at:

www.popsresources.com